ABCDEFGHI
JKLMNOPQ
RSTUVWXYZ

abcdefghijkl
mnopqrstuv
wxyz

❧

A·E·I·O·U·Y

Hornbooks
and
Inkwells

❧

VERLA KAY

Illustrated by
S. D. SCHINDLER

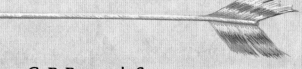

G. P. Putnam's Sons
An Imprint of Penguin Group (USA) Inc.

BIBLIOGRAPHY

Feldman, Ruth Tenzer. *Don't Whistle in School: The History of America's Public Schools.* Minneapolis: Lerner Publications, 2001.

Studer, Gerald C. *Christopher Dock Colonial Schoolmaster: The Biography and Writings of Christopher Dock.* Scottdale, Pa.: Herald Press, 1967.

Wickersham, James Pyle. *A History of Education in Pennsylvania: Private and Public, Elementary and Higher, from the Time the Swedes Settled on the Delaware to the Present Day.* Lancaster, Pa.: Inquirer Publishing Co., 1885.

G. P. PUTNAM'S SONS • A division of Penguin Young Readers Group. Published by The Penguin Group.
Penguin Group (USA) Inc., 375 Hudson Street, New York, NY 10014, U.S.A.
Penguin Group (Canada), 90 Eglinton Avenue East, Suite 700, Toronto, Ontario M4P 2Y3, Canada
(a division of Pearson Penguin Canada Inc).
Penguin Books Ltd, 80 Strand, London WC2R 0RL, England.
Penguin Ireland, 25 St. Stephen's Green, Dublin 2, Ireland (a division of Penguin Books Ltd.).
Penguin Group (Australia), 250 Camberwell Road, Camberwell, Victoria 3124, Australia
(a division of Pearson Australia Group Pty Ltd).
Penguin Books India Pvt Ltd, 11 Community Centre, Panchsheel Park, New Delhi - 110 017, India.
Penguin Group (NZ), 67 Apollo Drive, Rosedale, North Shore 0632, New Zealand
(a division of Pearson New Zealand Ltd).
Penguin Books (South Africa) (Pty) Ltd, 24 Sturdee Avenue, Rosebank, Johannesburg 2196, South Africa.
Penguin Books Ltd, Registered Offices: 80 Strand, London WC2R 0RL, England.

Design by Marikka Tamura. Text set in Grit Primer. The art was done with watercolor and gouache on elephant hide paper.
Library of Congress Cataloging-in-Publication Data
Kay, Verla.   Hornbooks and inkwells / Verla Kay ; illustrated by S. D. Schindler.   p. cm.   Summary: Two brothers spend a year attending a one-room schoolhouse on the frontier.
[1. Stories in rhyme. 2. Schools—Fiction. 3. Frontier and pioneer life—Fiction.] I. Schindler, S. D., ill. II. Title.   PZ83.K225Hor 2011   [E]—dc22   2010013070   ISBN 978-0-399-23870-3
10 9 8 7 6 5 4 3 2 1

To the special siblings in my life:
my sister and brother, Linda and Michael,
and my husband's siblings,
who have been like brothers and sisters to me, too—
Judy, Roger, Valerie and Larry.
Thank you for being in my life.—V.K.

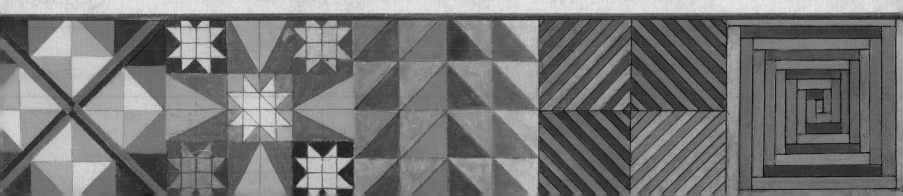

Squirrels scamper,
Acorns, munch.
Brothers skipping,
Gold leaves, CRUNCH!

One-room schoolhouse,
Ringing bell.
Chimney sparking,
Smoky smell.

Peter hollers,
"Time to go!
School is starting,
Don't ya know?"

John Paul racing.
"Cain't be late!"
Huffing, puffing,
"Peter, wait!"

 Sternly standing, Master greets.
Pairs of children, taking seats.

 Hardwood benches, musty smell.
Children scurry, final bell.

Girls' side, boys' side,
John in front.
Peter snickers,
"Yer a runt!"

John Paul bristles.
"Take that back!"
Brothers bicker,
Thick rod, THWACK!

Birch-bark paper,
Stripped from trees.
Hornbook, inkwell,
ABC's.

Daily lessons,
History.
Learning numbers,
One, two, three.

Recess, racing, wooden stilts.
Stepping, clomping, sideways tilts.

 Hard clay marbles, click, clack, click!
Ball of leather, hit with stick.

Recess over,
Psalms, recite.
Inkwells dripping,
Verses, write.

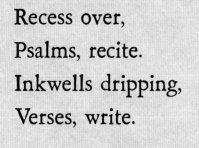

EEP! An error!
Peter sneers.
Four fists flying,
Grabbed by ears.

Wearing neck yokes,
Ridicule.
Children chanting,
"Yer a fool."

Nighttime, study,
Alphabet.
John Paul sighing,
"Cain't read yet."

Mother, hugging:
"You'll succeed."
John Paul labors,
Bible, read!

Mealtime munching, bread and cheese.
Snowflakes falling, small pond, freeze.

Wooden ice skates, spinning twirls.
Boys with red cheeks, laughing girls.

Big boys carry branches, sticks.
Woodstove crackles, warming bricks.

John Paul learns
Geography.
Peter winning
Spelling bee!

John Paul, outhouse—
"Need to go.
Where's the wood hook?
Someone's slow."

Peter playing,
Hook in hand.
Master scolding,
Reprimand.

Feather pen nib,
Sharpen tip.
Paper curling,
Ink pen, dip.

John Paul, window,
Daffodils.
End of daydreams,
Write with quills.

Pen tip dripping.
"Drat it! Hiss!"
Peter shows him.
"Here. Like this."

Printing letters,
A, B, C . . .
"Now I've got it!"
X, Y, Z.

John Paul jumping,
Pure delight.
"Lookit, Peter,
I kin write!"

School bell ringing,
Brothers flee.
John Paul puffing,
"Wait fer me!"

Author's Note

WHILE SEARCHING BOSTON'S PUBLIC LIBRARY, I FOUND AN INCREDIBLE, RARE BOOK: *Christopher Dock Colonial Schoolmaster — The Biography and Writings of Christopher Dock* by Gerald C. Studer. It includes minute details about the daily life at Christopher Dock's mid-1700s school, located in eastern Pennsylvania. Mr. Dock not only taught reading, writing, arithmetic, and religion (the four subjects taught in the 1700s), but he was also concerned with the morals, safety habits, physical and emotional health, courtesy, and social attitudes of his students—an extremely radical vision of teaching for the times. Also, he believed that children should not be beaten into submission but rather taught with love and understanding, with a rod or neck yoke used only as a last resort for unacceptable behavior in the classroom. His students were very lucky, indeed!

One of the most interesting things in the book was Mr. Dock's method for allowing students to use the outhouse. Many would ask to go but then stay outside and play rather than coming back. In order to stop this, he hung a big wooden hook by the door. When a student needed to go, the child would take the hook and no one else could leave the room until the hook was returned. If the hook wasn't returned in a timely manner, anyone waiting would complain loudly.

Although I've not found facts to support it, I do wonder if this "hook on the wall" was somehow involved in our current use of the phrase "playing hooky."

—V. K.